GENERATI*N GIRL ™

#1

New York,

Here We Come

By Melanie Stewart

A GOLD KEY PAPERBACK
Golden Books Publishing Company, Inc.
New York

This book is a work of fiction. Names, characters, places, and incidents are products of the author's imagination or are used fictitiously. Any resemblance to actual events or locales or persons, living or dead, is entirely coincidental.

A GOLD KEY Paperback Original

Golden Books Publishing Company, Inc.
888 Seventh Avenue
New York, NY 10106

ISBN: 0-307-23450-9

First GOLD KEY paperback printing May 1999

10   9   8   7   6   5

Printed in the U.S.A.

GENERATI*N GIRL ™

New York,
Here We Come

Chapter 1

Welcome to New York, Barbie!

"This will be your room, Barbie." Mrs. Jenner nudged the bedroom door open with her foot.

The blond teenager stepped inside and looked around.

Mrs. Jenner followed her in, carrying a stack of neatly folded linens and towels. "I did a little redecorating before you arrived," she said. "I packed up Scott's old sports trophies, took down his heavy metal posters, and added a few touches I felt a girl would appreciate." She waited a few moments for Barbie to take everything in — the futon bed, the retro sixties-style butterfly chair and fake leopard-skin throw pillows, the wrought-iron hat rack, and the giant CD tower. "Do you like it?" she asked.

"Like it?" asked Barbie. "I love it!" With a cry of delight, she threw her arms around Mrs. Jenner's neck and gave her a huge hug — towels and all. "This room is perfect. Totally perfect!"

Barbie stepped back, raised her arms toward the ceiling, and did a slow, dreamy pirouette. "It's so big and sunny and — oh-my-gosh!" Barbie stopped short and ran excitedly to the window. "What an amazing view!"

She pressed her nose to the pane. "Look at all of those buildings down there. There must be millions of them!"

Mrs. Jenner laughed. "Well, thousands, anyway."

Barbie stood on tiptoe to get a better look at the street below. She spied a group of kids on in-line skates go whizzing into the park across the way. They seemed no bigger than action figures. "How high up are we?" she asked.

"Fifteen floors."

"Awesome. Back in California everybody lives all spread out."

Mrs. Jenner smiled. "You're in New York now, honey. This is a tiny island with lots and lots of people. There's no room for anyone to spread out, so instead, everybody just spreads *up*." She put the sheets and towels on the bed and joined her bright and bubbly guest by the window.

"What river is that?" Barbie asked, pointing to a wide stretch of water beyond the park.

"The Hudson."

"Really?" said Barbie. Her blue eyes stared in wonder. In the slanting light of the evening sun, the wind-blown ripples of the river sparkled like sequins. "I didn't know it was so beautiful."

"It is lovely, isn't it?" Mrs. Jenner agreed, slipping an arm around Barbie's shoulder. "I never get tired of looking at it. It's always changing. I sometimes think the river has a personality of its own."

Barbie turned to face her new friend. "Mrs. Jenner?" she asked, "can I talk to you about something?"

"Of course," her host replied. "But only if you stop calling me 'Mrs. Jenner.' You're going to be spending a lot of time here with Sam and me while you're a student at International High School.

If you and I expect to be doing any serious girl talk, I think we ought to start out right now on a first-name basis, agreed?"

Barbie smiled appreciatively and nodded her head. She sensed she was going to like this twinkly-eyed woman with her direct and friendly manner.

"Excellent!" said Mrs. Jenner. "Now that we've got that settled, you can call me Terri."

"Okay, Mrs. Jen — oops! I mean, Terri."

Terri motioned to Barbie to sit down beside her on the window seat. "Okay," she said, straightening out her dress. "Now, what's on your mind?"

Barbie took a deep breath. "Well, it's not exactly one thing," she began. "It's a whole bunch of things."

"I'm listening," said Terri.

Barbie brushed back a strand of her long blond hair. "Okay," she said. "First off, I want you to know that I'm really, *really* excited about coming here to New York and staying with you and Mr. Jenner—"

"*Sam,*" interjected Terri.

"Sam," Barbie corrected herself. "And I'm really, *really* looking forward to starting high school

4

tomorrow. . . ." Barbie broke off and lowered her eyes.

Terri gave Barbie's hand a comforting squeeze. "But everything is a little overwhelming, right?" she asked softly.

Barbie looked up, impressed by Terri's ability to sense her feelings. "Uh-huh," she continued. "I know it sounds silly of me. I mean, I'm used to being independent. And I am fifteen years old. It's not like I haven't been anywhere or done anything."

Terri smiled. "Honey," she said, "everything you're feeling — from the thrills to the worries — is perfectly normal. Who wouldn't be a tangle of nerves in your position? You're coming to a big and strange city, boarding with old friends of your parents whom you hardly know, starting in a brand-new high school, and preparing to make new friends. I don't know what *you'd* call it, but in my book there's only one word for what you're doing, and that's 'brave.' "

Barbie's face brightened. "Thanks, Terri," she said. "That's so nice of you to say."

Terri leaned forward to stress her point. "I'm not

just saying this, you know. It's absolutely true. Besides, do you think you're the only teenager in New York with a case of the jitters on the night before her first day in a new high school?"

"I guess not."

"You guess right."

Barbie smiled sheepishly. "But do you really think I'll make friends fast? Friends are really important to me."

Terri snapped her fingers. "Just like that. You've got a wonderful personality. Every kid in school will want to be friends with you."

"You think?"

"I know."

Barbie heaved a deep sigh of relief. "You know, you're the next best thing to a mom," she said, and gave Terri another hug.

"Welcome to New York, Barbie," Terri said. "You know, with Scott away in the Peace Corps, it's good to have a youngster in the house again."

Long after the sun went down and the city lights blinked on, Barbie and Terri chatted together on the window seat.

At eight o'clock, the two of them left to have

dinner at Sam's restaurant, a few blocks away on Broadway. Barbie couldn't wait to see it. Her parents had told her that it had great food and such a cool atmosphere that famous writers and artists ate there all the time.

The restaurant, simply called Sam's, was more awesome than Barbie could have imagined. The walls were painted a deep burnt orange, and all the tables had crisp white tablecloths. On each table was a little candle that floated in water inside a round blue glass holder. The front doors of the restaurant were stained a beautiful shade of blue. On one wall was a mural of leaping dancers that an artist friend of Sam's had painted right onto the plaster. On the back wall was a display of award-winning photographs that Terri had taken when she'd worked as a photojournalist for *Time* and *Life* magazines.

The place was full of interesting-looking people having quiet conversations. There were bursts of laughter from time to time at different tables.

After a little while, Sam joined them, although he had to keep popping up to greet people. He was a bundle of energy — balding on top, but very trim and good-looking. It was obvious that his regular customers liked coming to the restaurant in part because of him.

Mr. Jenner had arranged a special meal for Barbie in honor of her arrival. There was pumpkin soup, fish with ginger sauce, and wild rice. For dessert, Barbie had blackberry ice cream and crunchy little cookies. It was about the best meal Barbie had ever had. And there she was, sitting and enjoying it with the *owner!*

Sam had to stay at the restaurant for hours longer, so Barbie and Terri returned home together. Barbie settled into her room and unpacked her suitcases. Then she switched on her laptop computer, linked up to the internet, and typed a short e-mail to her sister:

Tuesday at Midnight!
Dear Skipper:
I miss you and Stacie and Kelly sooo much. I know I just left you a day ago. But now there's a whole continent separating us, and I can't just walk into your room and hang out with you on the bed. Tomorrow I'm going to put your pictures up on the wall so I can look at your faces all the time.

New York, Here We Come

Mr. and Mrs. Jenner are sooo nice and sweet. I never expected I would feel at home so quickly. Oh, and this amazing thing happened while we were having dinner at Sam's restaurant. I mentioned to Sam that I'm interested in becoming an actress. And he told me he has a friend who's an agent, and that she can help me find acting jobs. Sam says she eats at his restaurant all the time. And he promised to tell her about me. Isn't that incredible?

Tomorrow is my first day of school. Actually, it's not a real school day. They call it "Zero Day." It's more like an opportunity for everybody to get together to meet everybody else. Isn't that neat?

I'm sooo excited. I can't believe that all of this is happening to me. And so fast.

I love you guys.

XOXOXOXOXOXOXOXOXOXOXOXOXOXOXOX

Please, please write back soon.

Your homesick sister,

Barbie

She clicked on the send button, and her e-mail went speeding through the night.

Chapter 2

Incident Underground

Barbie got up early the next morning to choose her clothes for school. Terri sat and watched patiently as Barbie tried on outfit after outfit.

"Ugh!"

"Too radical."

"Do you think this says 'out-of-towner'?"

"I feel like it needs *something*. I'm just not sure what."

Little by little Barbie's bed vanished under a mound of rejected items.

Terri glanced anxiously at the clock. "All these

outfits look great on you, honey," she said. "Just pick one."

Barbie sighed and rummaged through the pile again. Eventually, she settled on a pair of khaki Capri pants topped with a white tank top and a denim jacket.

"Fabulous!" Terri said. "Now let's have breakfast and send you on your way."

Two eggs, a toasted bagel, and half a pear later, Barbie was slinging on her backpack and flying out the door. She headed for the subway station on Broadway, three blocks away. That's where Terri had said she could catch a train that would take her directly to school.

It was a sunny September morning. On her way to the subway, Barbie was astonished to see how many people were already hustling and bustling about. There were men and women in snappy business suits. Parents pushing baby strollers. Workers making deliveries. Rosy-cheeked children squirming and yelling as they prepared to board yellow school buses. Barbie thrilled at the incredible energy of the place. She liked the sounds of the honking horns and rumbling trucks. And she liked the smells wafting from the bakery shops, pretzel carts, snack mobiles, and flower stands that she passed along her way. Though she was new to this city, she knew she wanted to be part of its daily rhythms and to experience it to the fullest.

As she descended the steps into the subway station, Barbie heard a noise that sounded like distant thunder. Almost immediately, the people around her quickened their pace. Hurrying through the turnstiles, Barbie located an empty spot on the crowded platform and stood staring down the tracks at the approaching train. It roared into the station like a sleek silver bull with glowing white eyes. The doors slid open and Barbie hopped on. She watched as the car filled up with people. There was just one empty seat left in the whole car. Amazingly, it was right in front of Barbie. Stenciled on the back of the seat were the words:

PRIORITY SEATING FOR PERSONS WITH DISABILITIES

What a nice rule, Barbie thought. She was glad she hadn't sat down without looking.

"Are you going to sit there?" an old man

inquired. Barbie noticed that he was walking with a cane.

"No, please take it," she said, stepping aside.

The old man smiled. "That's very kind of you."

Just then the subway doors closed, and the train lurched forward, pitching the old man off balance. Barbie grabbed his arm to save him from falling. But before the man could steady himself and sit down, a large man in a dirty T-shirt elbowed his way past and grabbed the seat.

Barbie was so astonished, she could hardly speak. "Excuse me, sir," she said. "This seat is taken."

The man threw Barbie a dark look. "You're right," he said. "It's taken by me!"

Barbie tried again. "Um, I'm really sorry. But I believe this seat is reserved for people with disabilities. You can see for yourself. It says so on the back."

The seated man ignored her.

"G'day, mate!" a girl's voice suddenly called out from behind. "You heard what my friend here said. That's not your seat!"

Barbie turned and saw a wiry, athletic girl with long blond ponytails who had a pair of in-line skates slung across her shoulder. From her accent, Barbie guessed that the girl was from Australia. She said "G'day" and "mate" just the way the character in the movie *Crocodile Dundee* did.

The train was picking up speed. The *clickety-clack* of the tracks was nearly deafening.

The seat-thief stared silently ahead as if nothing had happened.

"Hey, I'm not blind, you know," shouted the out-spoken girl. "I saw it all. While this girl was helping out this gent, you stole his seat." She edged her way forward, stopping right beside Barbie.

"Honest, sir," Barbie said to the clench-jawed squatter. "I would have let you have it. But this nice man with the cane asked for it first. And he needs it more than we do."

The large man looked up at Barbie and her new-found ally. "You girls don't own this seat," he grumbled. "And neither does he." He pointed to the elderly man.

"Let him have it, girls," the old gentleman said wearily. "I don't want to cause any trouble. I can stand."

"No way!" exclaimed the Aussie. "Don't you

worry. I'm gonna get your seat back." She stared at the man in the dirty T-shirt. "How about it, mate? You gonna let this nice man sit down?"

"Who are you? The seat police?" the trouble-maker snorted. "Why don't you mind your own business?"

With a screech of the wheels, the train began slowing down for the next stop.

The girl with the accent took a deep breath and yelled above the noise. "Listen up, people! This man in front of me stole a seat from somebody who needed it!"

All at once the chatter in the car ceased. All eyes in the car focused on the heavyset man.

"Shame on you!" scolded a lady with white hair.

"I think you ought to get up, buddy," said a muscular man standing near the double doors.

A young woman three seats down stood up. "Here, sir," she said to the elderly man. "You can have my seat!"

With everyone giving him such cold stares, the large man grew increasingly uncomfortable. As the train groaned to a halt in the next station, the doors sprang open, and the man jumped up. "Bunch of busybodies!" he shouted, and stormed off the train. "That's what's wrong with this country!"

The old man reclaimed his seat with a grateful smile, and everybody in the subway car cheered.

What a wonderful moment, Barbie thought. People rallying to help people. She turned to share it with her spunky subway companion. But the girl with the blond ponytails was no longer beside her. She, too, had apparently slipped out of the car.

Shaking her head, Barbie smiled to herself. New York really was full of all kinds of people. And for every rude one, it looked like there were a whole bunch of caring and good ones.

Chapter 3

First Friend

About ten minutes later, Barbie's train pulled into the Chambers Street station, and a swarm of passengers, Barbie among them, piled out of the cars. The platform was very long. Barbie wasn't exactly sure which way was out. But the sea of people around her seemed to be moving in one general direction, so she decided to join the flow.

Halfway down the platform she stopped to listen to a trio of guitarists serenading the crowd in Spanish. When they finished singing, the audience of spectators and passersby burst into applause.

A few appreciative people tossed coins into an open guitar case at the musicians' feet. Barbie searched the bottom of her backpack for some loose change and dropped it into the case.

Barbie was feeling quite pleased with herself. She had completed her first subway ride ever as a New Yorker, and she had done it all alone. Now the big question was, how would she get from here to school? She took out the "Zero Day" brochure that she'd stuffed into her pocket and glanced at the directions:

Exit from subway onto Chambers Street.
Walk one block south to Warren Street.
Head two blocks west until you reach West Street.
Look for a big white stone building.
Enter via tunnel under West Street.
(See page 3 for street map.)

As Barbie flipped through the brochure she was thankful to have such detailed instructions. There was only one problem. Page 3 of her brochure — the page with the map on it — was missing! She remembered hearing Terri say that I. H. was located somewhere in the Wall Street area, near the southern tip of the island. But when it came to New York City geography Barbie didn't know north from south or east from west. To make matters worse, she still hadn't a clue as to which way was the best way out of the subway station. Maybe it was time to ask someone for help.

Barbie scanned the crowd for a friendly face. Amid the parade of no-nonsense business types were groups of bright, cool-looking kids. They were laughing, singing, jumping around, vibrating to their own inner beats. She picked out one, a girl about her own age, who had a long, dark brown braid hanging down her back.

"Excuse me!" called Barbie, with a little wave. But the squeal of an incoming train drowned out her words. The girl walked right by, unaware that Barbie was trying to attract her attention.

"Darn!" Barbie muttered.

Her eyes followed the girl down the platform. The girl had a book bag slung casually over one shoulder. The crest on the bag had the words INTERNATIONAL HIGH SCHOOL on it. That was a good sign. Barbie decided to tag along behind her. This girl was sure to lead her to school.

Then something happened. It was over so quickly, Barbie almost didn't catch it: a flash of long blond hair, someone flying past her, and — *OOF!* It was the Australian girl that Barbie had encountered earlier. She had sideswiped the girl with the backpack.

"Sorry, mate! You all right?" she called back as she pumped along on her skates toward the staircase.

"Not any thanks to you!" yelled the girl, rubbing her elbow.

Barbie caught up to her. "You okay?" she asked.

"I suppose I am okay," said the girl in a cute foreign accent, possibly French. "I just wish people would look where they are going." She hitched her book bag onto her shoulder.

"I'm just glad you didn't get hurt," said Barbie. "It's hard for someone to stop on skates."

"I guess so, but I do not wear mine in the subway." She smiled at Barbie.

"Um, can I ask you a question?" said Barbie.

"But of course," said the girl.

"I see you have an I. H. backpack. Do you go there?"

"Yes," replied the girl. "Starting today."

"Well, I do, too. And I'm pretty lost. I don't know what to do when I get upstairs. My 'Zero Day' guide is missing the page with the map."

The girl laughed. "My 'Zero Day' guide is missing also the page with the map!" she said. "I was hoping to ask *you* how to go!"

Now they both laughed. "A lot of good we're going to do each other," said Barbie. "Now what?"

"Now we figure it out together." The girl stretched out her hand to Barbie. "My name is Lara," she said. "Lara Morelli-Strauss."

Barbie shook her hand.

"I'm Barbie Roberts. I'm an exchange student from California. Where do you come from? Are you French?"

The girl chuckled. "Well, not exactly."

"What do you mean?" asked Barbie.

"Well, I am a true European. My mother is Italian. My father, he is German. And I was born in Paris while my father was teaching at the Sorbonne there. I have lived in three countries since I was born."

"Wow!" said Barbie.

"So," continued Lara, "it is of course natural that

I speak many languages. I am a girl with — how do you say it? — a many-cultures background."

Barbie found herself fascinated by Lara. She'd lived in three foreign countries and she could speak several foreign languages — including English! Barbie imagined that she could learn a lot from a worldly girl like this.

"Look," said Lara. "There is a police officer. We can ask him where to go."

There was indeed an officer standing near the exit staircase. The badge sewn onto his sleeve said METROPOLITAN TRANSIT AUTHORITY POLICE. The girls waited until he had finished giving directions to a woman in a suit, then asked him how to walk to International High School.

"Easy as pie," he said. "Go up the stairs, hang a quick left, hang a right at the next corner, walk two blocks, then — bingo! — you're there!"

"Thanks!" said Barbie with a big smile.

As they walked up the stairs, Lara looked very confused. "What was this man saying? We are eating pie? And then we are hanging things? I don't understand."

Barbie smiled. "I guess a lot of the English that

Americans speak every day isn't exactly in the books."

As Lara walked up the steps, Barbie noticed a big box bumping against her legs. Barbie began to wonder about it. It wasn't the usual kind of thing kids took to school.

"What do you have in there?" Barbie asked. "It looks like it weighs a million pounds!"

"It is not so heavy," Lara replied over her shoulder. "But it is very important to me." When they arrived at the top of the stairs, Lara rested the box on top of a brass fireplug. Then she undid the clasps. "I am going to give you a present," she said. "A little one, to thank you for helping me."

"Oh, no, you don't have to!" said Barbie.

"But I want to," said Lara.

Barbie peered over Lara's shoulder into the box. She saw neat rows of tubes of paint and a selection of good-quality paintbrushes. It looked as if the contents of the box had cost a fortune.

In a special compartment in the lid of the box was a set of beautiful hand-painted postcards. Lara took one out and handed it to Barbie. It was a scene of Paris at night. Barbie could tell because she recognized the Eiffel Tower in the background.

"Lara, you didn't paint this yourself, did you?" Barbie asked.

"Of course."

"This is beautiful! It looks like it could be in a museum. You're really an amazing artist."

"It is nothing."

"Lara," said Barbie, "I just don't feel right taking this from you. It's way too special. You don't want to just give something like this away."

"I most certainly do. Besides," Lara continued, "I have so many of them. If I want more, I paint more. Please, Barbie, I want you to have it."

Barbie was deeply touched. "Thank you," she said. "I'm going to keep it forever."

Lara closed the box. It was time to get moving if they were going to get to school on time. On the way there, they exchanged stories about their first experiences as New Yorkers. By the time they'd reached their destination, Barbie couldn't have been happier. Her wish had come true: She had made her first new friend.

Chapter 4

Lara's Gamble

At West Street, Barbie and Lara joined the crush of kids funneling into the student tunnel. The tunnel was brightly lit and had gently sloping access ramps and a special wheelchair lift for the disabled. Every few feet along the walls were large, polished mirrors with painted faces of teenagers from around the world.

Barbie gave a tug on Lara's arm. "This is so cool!" she said, staring at each portrait as they filed past. "It's like looking into a mirror. Only, each time you do, you see two faces looking back — your own and the one in the painting." She turned to her friend. "What do think, Lara? Do you like this stuff?"

"It's fantastic!" said Lara, giving each syllable a lilting French twist. "I love everything. The colors. The realistic faces. The way we become part of the pictures." She made a sweeping gesture with her hand. "This is why I decided to come to I. H. You would not find such artwork in my old school."

"You're kidding?"

Lara shook her head. "I am not kidding you."

"C'mon," Barbie teased. "I thought Paris was the art capital of the world."

"It is. But my school in Paris was very strict. Everything had to be done by the rules."

"Gee, why did you go there?"

"My family has its own rules, too. My father chose it for me because some famous artist he knew taught there. I know he meant well. But I didn't want to paint like that artist. I wanted to paint like me. But I wasn't allowed. Artistic freedom was against the rules."

"Couldn't you say something to your parents?"

Lara heaved a deep sigh. "I tried. I begged them

to send me somewhere else. My mother said yes in a second. But my father — he refused. He said he thought it would do me good to learn to paint like this famous artist. I said no. He said yes. So, finally, I decided to make him — how do you say it? — a gamble."

"You mean, a bet?"

"Yes, that is it — a bet."

"What about?"

"I bet him I could learn to paint like this artist in one year, win the art prize, and get the highest grades in school. I told him that if I didn't succeed, I would stay in his school and complain no more."

"And if you won?"

"Then my father would have to let me pick whatever school I wanted."

Barbie whistled softly. "Wow! Some bet! You were really risking a lot."

"Perhaps."

"No, I mean it. I'm really impressed."

"Do not be," Lara said. "I had no other choice. Art means everything to me."

Barbie marveled at her friend. She couldn't recall

anyone her own age who cared half as much about anything as Lara cared about art.

Lara adjusted the position of her book bag. "The rest you can probably guess. I won my bet, and when my year was up, I applied to I. H.

"Of all the schools I considered, this one attracted me most. Here, I can do whatever art I want — in whatever style I like." Lara's voice softened. "Here, I can be free to be myself."

"And your father's okay about this? Your choice, I mean."

"Yes. He must. Because a lucky thing happened that — poof! — changed everything."

Barbie eyes widened. "What could be luckier than getting your wish?"

"Only this. You see, my father is a university professor. And just when I learned the art prize was mine, he was offered a job here in New York. At first, he thought he should not take it. But then when I was accepted into I. H., he said yes. So instead of just me coming here, my whole family moved here."

"Unbelievable!" said Barbie. "I'm so jealous! My mom and dad are working in China. The rest of my family is back in California. And I'm staying here with friends of my parents."

"Your parents — they are on vacation in China?"

"Actually, no. They're working there. They're on an archaeological dig."

"Ah, I see. That is interesting work, no?"

"It is," Barbie agreed. "I just wish that we could all be together now — like your family."

A funny look crept into Lara's eyes. "I know exactly how you are feeling," she said. "It is very sad to be apart. But, of course, it is not always perfection when a family is together."

Barbie was puzzled by this remark, but she decided it would be prying to ask Lara exactly what she'd meant, so she just walked along silently with her new friend, gazing at the pictures.

Upon exiting the tunnel, the girls were greeted by two school officials with clipboards in hand. One of the adults was a short, peppy woman with light brown hair and dark, expressive eyebrows that set off startlingly green, don't-miss-a-trick eyes. Above the pocket of her suit she wore a large name tag that read:

HI, I'M PRINCIPAL SIMMONS!
I DON'T BITE!

The other school official was a tall, bespectacled man with a dimpled chin and a wispy pencil mustache. He had shiny, well-groomed black hair that was parted down the middle. From the condition of his red, watery eyes, he seemed to be suffering from a bad case of allergies. His name tag — unlike the principal's — sported no jokes. It read simply ASSISTANT PRINCIPAL MERLIN in rigidly straight hand-printed letters.

Assistant Principal Merlin sneezed explosively. "Hello," he sniffled at Barbie and Lara. "Welcome to 'Zero Day.'"

Barbie gave him a bright smile and said, "My name is Barbie Roberts."

"Pardon me, Oliver," Principal Simmons smiled at Barbie. "I recall reading your application essay. You have three younger sisters. And you're interested in acting, aren't you?"

"That's amazing!" replied Barbie. "How did you

remember all that?"

Principal Simmons tapped her head and laughed. "Good little gray cells, I suppose."

Barbie shook the principal's hand. "I'm so happy to be here, Principal Simmons."

"Well, we're so delighted to have you." She glanced down at her list. "You're going to be in the Welcome Group with Mr. Toussaint in Room 555. I see from your schedule that he'll also be your English teacher. I know you're going to love him."

Then Lara stepped up and introduced herself. "You're going to be in the Creative Arts Welcome Group, dear," Principal Simmons said. "That's Mr. Harris, in Room 241. He'll be your art teacher."

Assistant Principal Merlin checked both girls off his clipboard. Then Principal Simmons directed them toward a bunch of tables set up on the playing field adjoining the school. "You can pick up your box brunches and other goodies over there. Sit wherever you like. There are benches all around. Eat. Mix. Have fun. When you hear the bell, go directly to your Welcome Groups." She smiled graciously, then beckoned to the next students in line to step forward.

Barbie and Lara found a picnic bench that overlooked the river. They ate their meals in the shadow of the World Trade Center, whose lofty twin towers split the morning light like shafts of a giant tuning fork. Soon they were joined by two other kids — a girl and a boy. It quickly became apparent that the newcomers didn't know one another. So Barbie decided to break the ice. She ripped open a bag of nacho chips and spread it flat like a plate on the table. Then she motioned for everyone to dig in. As everybody crunched away, she handed out napkins and introduced herself and Lara. Then the two others introduced themselves in turn. The girl was named Ana Suarez, and the boy was Randall Zaleski.

Ana was a vivacious Mexican-American with lustrous black hair and piercing brown eyes. She had the kind of features that were naturally attractive and rarely needed makeup. Barbie guessed that she probably worked out a lot. She had strong, well-tanned arms and shoulders, calloused hands, and close-clipped fingernails. Sure enough, Ana mentioned a few minutes later that she was a serious competitive athlete. She'd been training for months for the upcoming Central Park Triathlon, in which she planned to participate in three different sports: swimming, running, and bicycling.

As for the boy, Barbie liked him instantly. He had big brown puppy dog eyes and a shy, vulnerable expression that made Barbie instinctively want to take care of him. He wore patched black jeans, droopy black socks, black work boots (shoelaces untied), and a worn black shirt. His hair was hopeless. Huge, unruly tufts popped up this way and that, and several long strands seemed permanently draped over one eye. He blushed as he introduced himself to the girls and mumbled his words so badly that he was forced to repeat them. When Barbie offered him another chip, their fingers accidentally touched, and he blushed a second time.

Randall didn't speak much after that. Instead, he pulled out a notepad and hunched over it, drawing amazing pictures of comic book-type superheroes. Barbie could see Lara edge closer to Randall, watching every line, every shading, every swirl he made. Barbie could almost hear Lara saying to herself, "Yes, this is why I decided to come to I. H."

Just as they finished eating, the bell rang. It was time for them to head off to their Welcome Groups. Barbie and Lara quickly made plans to meet after school by the sculpture in front of the building. As Barbie waited in line to enter the ground floor, she thought she saw a familiar figure out of the corner of her eye. She glanced over her shoulder. There, on the road leading to the teachers' parking lot, was a girl with long blond ponytails, doing acrobatic maneuvers on in-line skates. *Could it be?* Barbie wondered. Was it the girl who had helped her on the subway? She blinked and looked again. But the mystery girl had vanished like a mirage.

Perplexed, Barbie raced up to her fifth-floor classroom. She did not want to be late for Mr. Toussaint.

Chapter 5

Mr. Toussaint

Barbie took a seat by the window. She could see practically all of New York Harbor and the magnificent Statue of Liberty in the hazy distance. By the time the hall bell rang, signaling the start of Welcome Groups, about twenty-five kids had drifted into the room. Mr. Toussaint left no doubt in anyone's mind about what subject he taught. The room was covered with pictures of famous writers, quotes from famous books, clippings from the latest book reviews, and stirring lines of poetry.

Mr. Toussaint sat perched on the front edge of

his desk, waiting for everyone to settle down. He was a tall African American with slightly graying hair, a high forehead, and warm, sensitive eyes. He was elegantly dressed in a navy blue suit, white shirt, maroon suspenders, and a red silk tie. Barbie thought he had incredible presence. He didn't move a muscle as the students wound down their chatter, yet he seemed to be aware of everything that was going on.

Gradually all heads swung forward, and all eyes fixed on him like needles on a compass. The class hushed.

"Good!" said Mr. Toussaint in a deep voice. He unbuttoned his jacket and tossed it casually onto the back of his chair. "Let us begin, then!" He jumped to his feet, went to the blackboard, and wrote:

HENRI TOUSSAINT

"That's my name," he said. "I'll be your English teacher this year. We'll be meeting every day, second period. I also have two other jobs here at I. H. I'm the sophomore class adviser and the adviser to the school newspaper. So if you have any problems, come see me in my office — Room 502. If you do, you'll notice that my office has no door. There's a reason for that. I removed it. I don't believe in closed doors. If you're there to talk to me, I'm there to listen." He paused, jiggling chalk in hand. "Everyone got that?"

The class nodded.

"Terrific!"

Mr. Toussaint turned to face the students. "Now I should say a few words about I. H. As you know, this is a brand-new school. So new, in fact, that we haven't quite got all the bugs out of the building. You may have noticed, for example, that the escalators aren't working yet—"

"I got stuck in the elevator!" one student shouted out.

"Me, too!" called another.

"And there's no hot water in the girls' bathroom," moaned a third.

Mr. Toussaint raised a hand and laughed. "Okay, okay. I hear you. Try to be patient, though. Principal Simmons is doing everything she can to get all systems up and running in the next couple of weeks."

"Couple of weeks?" croaked a skinny boy in the

back. "Gimme a break! You mean I've got to climb five flights of stairs for a couple of weeks?"

The whole class groaned.

"Take it easy," Mr. Toussaint said. Again he raised a calming hand, and again the students fell silent. "Let's get real for a moment. This school isn't just about a building. This school is made up of teachers and students working together for a common purpose." He furrowed his brow. "Some people say a public school like I. H. can't work — that the only good education is one you can buy. We don't believe that here. We believe you're here because you want to learn. More importantly, we believe you're here because you want to learn from one another."

Mr. Toussaint paused and gazed out over the classroom. "Let me take a quick poll. How many of you are from New York?"

About a dozen hands went up.

"How many from other parts of the U.S.?"

Five kids, including Barbie, raised their hands.

"Okay. How many of you come from other countries?"

Seven arms waved in the air.

"Terrific," Mr. Toussaint said. He leaped to the

board again. "You may have seen the school motto on the sculpture out front. If not, here it is." He dashed out eight words in chalk:

MANY PEOPLES, MANY CULTURES, ONE HEART, ONE WORLD

"We take these words very seriously here," he said. "You're what makes this school great. Your ideas. Your drive. Your dreams. I'd gladly climb fifteen flights of stairs for the privilege of teaching kids like you." He wheeled around. "Now, does anyone have any more complaints about the building not being ready?"

The room was silent. Barbie was spellbound. She'd never heard a teacher talk like this before.

"Good," Mr. Toussaint said. "Now let's get down to business." There was a mischievous gleam in his eyes. "I need two volunteers. How about one boy and one girl?"

The students shrank in their seats.

"C'mon," Mr. Toussaint persisted. "I promise not to saw anyone in half."

Barbie hesitantly raised her hand. If she was going

to be an actress, she had to learn to be comfortable in front of big groups.

"Excellent — that's one!" said Mr. Toussaint. "Now, I need a boy."

No boy volunteered.

Mr. Toussaint put his hands on his hips. "What a bunch of wimps! Okay, how about another girl, then?"

Sitting directly across from Barbie was a girl with cascades of curly auburn hair. She lifted her hand.

"Good — another brave girl!" He motioned for both girls to step up to the front of the room.

Barbie was a little nervous. She didn't know what to expect.

"I presume both of you young ladies have names?" Mr. Toussaint said.

"Barbie Roberts," Barbie replied.

"And I'm Chelsie Peterson," the auburn-haired girl added shyly. She spoke with an unmistakably high-class English accent.

"My pleasure," Mr. Toussaint said with a tiny bow. He took off his tie and handed it to Barbie.

"Here, Barbie," he said. "I'd like you to help me with an experiment. I want you to tie this in a perfect bow around Chelsie's neck. Do it slowly, please, so everyone can see how you do it."

"Um, okay," said Barbie.

"Now, everybody, watch!" Mr. Toussaint instructed the class.

Barbie turned toward Chelsie. Her classmate had a sweet, oval-shaped face, an unblemished pearly-white complexion, and lovely hazel eyes. Barbie had to brush back masses of perfect curls in order to slip Mr. Toussaint's tie around her long neck.

"Ooh — it tickles," giggled Chelsie as Barbie fashioned a bow.

"Good job, girls," Mr. Toussaint said, applauding softly. "Now, I'd like both of you to stay up here while everybody else takes out a pen and paper."

Groans rippled through the classroom.

"I didn't know we were supposed to have notebooks today!"

"I've got a bad case of writer's cramp."

"My dog ate my pen."

"Nice try," Mr. Toussaint said, wagging his finger

at the class. "But you're not getting off that easily." He gestured to the skinny boy in the back. "Young man, what's your name?"

"Fletcher, sir."

"Good. Fletcher, would you kindly pass out some writing materials to anyone who needs them? You'll find paper and pens in the cabinet behind you."

Fletcher nodded and did Mr. Toussaint's bidding. Seconds later, Mr. Toussaint called for silence again. "I hope that all of you were paying attention while Barbie made her bow," he began. "Because now I want you to write down exactly how she did it, step by step." He paused. "After you're finished, we'll have Barbie follow your directions to the letter. We'll see if anyone here can write good instructions."

"I don't get it," said one boy.

"What's the big deal?" asked a girl.

"Piece of cake," quipped another.

"Let's just wait and see," Mr. Toussaint said dryly.

The students threw themselves into the task with enthusiasm. Each wanted to be the one who met Mr. Toussaint's challenge. In the end, though, the assignment proved a lot harder than they had anticipated. Barbie tried to follow the directions her fellow students had written as closely as she could. In some cases, the bow became an unrecognizable knot. In other cases, only half a bow was produced. In still others, the knot simply fell apart.

"Gosh," gasped one girl after all the different versions had been tried. "Nobody did it. I really thought this was going to be easy."

Mr. Toussaint strode to the board again. "Unclear writing is always easy!" he said. "Clear writing is always hard. What makes clear writing hard is that it forces you to be honest with yourself. You must always ask yourself, 'What do I really mean to say?'"

He turned back to the board and wrote:

WRITING = HONESTY = TRUTH

"In this class," he explained, "you will write often, you will write honestly, and you will write truthfully. And when you do this, you will also feel your own power as individuals. I want you to say this aloud." He tapped the words on the board.

"Writing equals honesty equals truth," a few voices called out sheepishly.

"Louder!" Mr. Toussaint ordered.

The chorus deepened. "WRITING EQUALS HONESTY EQUALS TRUTH."

Mr. Toussaint cupped his ear. "I still can't hear you!"

"WRITING EQUALS HONESTY EQUALS TRUTH!" yelled the students at the top of their lungs. By now they were grinning from ear to ear. They had never had a teacher who had actually asked them to shout in class.

Just then the door in the rear opened, and Mr. Merlin poked his head in. "Dear me," he said. "Is everything all right in here, Mr. Toussaint? I heard loud noises." Mr. Merlin sneezed loudly.

"Everything's fine, Mr. Merlin," Mr. Toussaint said. "We were just — uh — clearing our throats."

Mr. Merlin wiped his nose. "Ah, yes. I see. Well, all right, then — carry on." He sniffled his way back out into the hall.

Mr. Toussaint looked at the clock. "Okay, it's eleven-thirty. We only have twenty minutes left before I have to send you home. Right now, I want each of you to work with a partner. For the rest of the period, I want you to act like reporters and interview one another. Then, for homework tonight—"

Huge groans.

"For homework tonight, you will write a composition on your partner's life story, and your partner, in turn, will write one on yours. Do not — I repeat *do not* — go over one hundred and fifty words."

"Is fifty okay?" Fletcher called out.

"Only if they're brilliant," retorted Mr. Toussaint. "Okay, now, here's the good part. As an incentive, I intend to print the two best compositions from each of my classes in the first issue of the school newspaper."

Although a few kids continued to grumble, most actually seemed excited by the prospect of having their writing published for the whole school to read.

Barbie and Chelsie looked at one another.

"Partners?" asked Barbie.

"Partners," said Chelsie.

Then the two girls sat down and frantically

scribbled notes about each other's lives. Barbie asked Chelsie if she wanted to go with her to meet Lara after school, but Chelsie apologized and said she couldn't. She said that her mum hadn't been feeling well lately and that she had to take care of her while her dad was away on business. At the bell, the two girls quickly exchanged phone numbers just in case they needed to contact one another about their compositions.

Barbie dashed down the stairs and out the front doors toward the huge bronze sculpture of young people balancing a globe of the world on their finger tips.

She spotted Lara about twenty yards up the bike-and-skating path. Something seemed to have really upset her, because she was jumping up and down and screaming things loudly in French. Barbie touched her friend's shoulder and tried to calm her down. "What's wrong?" she asked.

Lara pointed up the path. "That girl," she sputtered. "She has stolen my paint box."

Barbie looked. There, in the distance, was a blond girl with long ponytails skating up the promenade. She had Lara's wooden paint box in her arms.

Barbie's heart sank. There was no question about who the girl was this time. It was definitely the Australian. None of this made any sense to Barbie. How could the courageous girl she'd met that morning also be a thief?

Chapter 6

"Stop, Thief!?"

Lara was hopping mad. "My postcards and paints are in there!" she cried, starting out after the Aussie.

"There's no way you're gonna catch her," said Barbie. "She's too far ahead. Besides, she's on skates. You're wearing platforms."

"That box is worth about two hundred dollars!"

A gust of wind sweeping off the river blew a pair of seagulls overhead. For a moment they hung motionless in the air, fighting the head wind and calling to each other in shrill voices. They studied the two girls with mild curiosity. Then they tipped their wings and shot out over the water again.

Lara took a deep breath. Within moments, the fiery flush disappeared from her face. The tenseness in her eyes softened, and her expression returned to its cool, composed state. Lara was once more in control.

"Want to tell me what happened?" Barbie asked.

Lara gave a shrug. "There is not much to say. Mr. Harris let us out early, so I came directly here. I left my things for five minutes to get a drink of water. When I returned, that girl" — she pointed to the tiny retreating figure — "was skating off with my paints." Lara furrowed her brows. "I must inform Principal Simmons," she said. "And then Principal Simmons must call the police."

"No!" Barbie blurted out loudly — so loudly, in fact, that she actually startled herself.

"Why not?" questioned Lara. "That girl must be reported — or she will steal again."

A hundred thoughts went racing through Barbie's mind. But they all boiled down to one thing: Barbie didn't believe in her heart of hearts that a girl who was kind enough to stand up for a disabled person on the subway could ever steal from anyone.

"I know this is going to sound totally off the wall," said Barbie. "But I don't think we should involve the police — at least, not yet."

"What are you saying? That we should do a big nothing?"

Suddenly Barbie wished she had kept her mouth shut. She had an awful feeling that she was digging herself into a very deep hole. "No, I didn't mean that," she said, flapping her hands as if to brush the problem away. "All I meant was that it's okay to tell Principal Simmons if you want, but—"

"But what?"

"It's just that I think there has to be some kind of explanation for this. I know that girl, a little. And I just know she isn't a bad person — honest!"

Lara scrutinized Barbie carefully. "How do you know this?"

Barbie then proceeded to tell Lara the story of her subway adventure. After she'd finished, Lara thought for a while, then said, "You are very nice, Barbie. You think people are very nice, too. I do not think people are always good. But somehow you make me feel I should try to think this."

"Lara," said Barbie, "would you let me try to find this girl and figure out why she took your paints?"

"I guess so," Lara said. "But soon I will have to go to the principal's office — just in case this girl is not as nice as you think."

"Okay," said Barbie. "That's fair."

By this time, it was nearly one o'clock, and Barbie could hear a low rumbling in the pit of her stomach. She could no longer think about how she was going to locate the Australian girl or what she would say once she found her. She could only think about one thing.

"Wouldn't you just love a slice of pepperoni pizza?" she said. "Or an extra large order of cheese fries? Or a bacon burger with onion rings? Or a large chef salad?"

"Are you hungry?" asked Lara.

"Hungry? I'm starved!" Barbie exclaimed.

Lara broke into a grin. "Okay," she said. "Let us find a restaurant before you drop!"

They didn't have to venture far. Only a block from school Barbie discovered the munch-'n'-

lunch hangout of her dreams. It was called Eatz. From the street, the restaurant didn't look like much. But on the inside, the place was jumping with serious energy. Eatz was the size of two railroad cars crunched together in an "L." Tattered orange vinyl booths ran along the walls. An old-fashioned jukebox blasted out rock-and-roll favorites.

Lara and Barbie sat down in a window booth and studied the yellowing eight-page menu. Barbie couldn't decide whether she wanted a Turkey Deli Sandwich or an Ultimate Cobb Salad. She kept changing her mind, flipping back and forth between the sandwich and salad sections, until Lara grew exasperated and practically yelled at her to pick something. Red-faced, Barbie decided to go for a burger, while Lara ordered a garden salad and a cup of mushroom soup.

The restaurant was packed with I. H. students. Barbie spotted Ana, and also Randall. As Barbie tore into her burger, Lara lifted a fork and pointed in the direction of a slender African-American girl who was talking animatedly with a friend.

"See that girl?" Lara said. "Her name's Nichelle

Williams. She was in my Welcome Group. She is very smart, I think." Barbie watched as Lara lowered her fork, neatly speared a slice of cucumber, and chewed it thoroughly before swallowing. "She talked about African art and American jazz. Whenever she spoke, she said interesting things." Lara chased a slippery cherry tomato around her plate. "I hope I can get to know her better."

After they finished eating, the two girls lingered at Eatz for more than an hour, drinking sodas, listening to music, and watching two cute boys juggling tennis balls in time to jukebox selections. Lara dubbed them the "Pants Boys" because they wore baggy pants that hung dangerously low on their hips.

Suddenly, Barbie remembered her English assignment. She wanted to write something really good for Mr. Toussaint. Lara wanted to stay to talk with Nichelle, so Barbie reluctantly said good-bye and hopped a train back uptown.

Nobody was home when she walked in. But two messages were waiting for her on the answering machine. One was from Chelsie, who asked Barbie to call her later that night so they could double-check the facts in their stories. The second was from Selma Devine, Sam's agent friend.

Barbie's heart skipped a beat. What could Selma Devine want? She scribbled down the agent's number on a pad and took it into her bedroom. Then she kicked off her shoes, got comfortable on her bed, picked up the phone, and dialed.

The phone rang and rang and rang. Just as Barbie was about to hang up, a raspy female voice came on the line. "Devine Talent."

"Selma Devine, please?"

"You're talking to her, sweetie. What can I do for you?"

Barbie sat bolt upright. "Ms. Devine?"

"Selma, hon."

"All right, Selma. This is Barbie Roberts."

"Hey there, Barbie! I was hoping you'd call back soon. How are you? You're the girl who's staying with Sam and Terri, right?"

"Uh-huh. At least while I'm going to I. H."

"Marvelous!" exclaimed the agent. "They're real gems, that pair. Just darling, darling people. They don't make 'em like that anymore."

"I've only known them for a couple of days, but

I love them already," Barbie said. "They've made me feel so at home and so special."

"Fabulous!" replied Selma. "Glad to hear it." The agent cleared her throat in a thoroughly businesslike manner. "Listen, sweetie," she said. "I guess you're wondering why I called?"

Barbie gripped the phone tighter. "Um, yes."

"Well, Sam tells me that you're serious about pursuing an acting career."

"I am. I really am, Selma. It's been my dream forever."

The agent sighed. "Unfortunately, it's practically every other young girl's dream, too. Look, before we go any further, I want you to know something. I'm a real straight-shooter. I always tell people the truth. And I want you to know right now that acting isn't easy. It isn't half as glamorous as it seems. And only a few people ever make it to the top. You've gotta have talent, but in my book, guts and determination count for even more." She paused to let all of this sink in. "Do you understand me?"

"Perfectly."

"Okay. Have you ever had any professional acting experience?"

"Some," answered Barbie.

"Like what, for instance?"

Barbie had the list ready in her mind. "Well, I starred in four school plays. I played Heidi in the Malibu Summer Theater Festival. I was Dorothy in *The Wizard of Oz* on a local cable television show. And for the last two years I was a magician's assistant to Dundarr the Magnificent at the Malibu Mall's Children's Christmas Festival."

"These were all back in California?"

"Uh-huh."

"Hmm," mused Selma. "Not too shabby. Okay then, Barbie. I may just have something for you."

"You mean it?"

"Wouldn't say it if I didn't."

"Oh-my-gosh!" shrieked Barbie ecstatically. "A real New York acting job!"

"Whoa! Hold it right there. We're not talking jobs yet, only auditions. So don't get your hopes up. Besides, I've got to meet you first, look you over, and see what kind of parts you can play. Can you meet me at Sam's Thursday night?"

"Absolutely!"

"Good, I've got another call coming in. So we'll discuss this some more then. Okay?"

"Okay."

"See you tomorrow."

"See you," echoed Barbie, hanging up.

She lay on the bed and pinched herself. Was she dreaming, or not?

After dinner, Barbie went to her room to write her composition. At first, she found it difficult to concentrate. She kept thinking about Lara's paint box. Maybe she did put too much faith in the goodness of people. To change her mood, she put on her CD player, plugged in her earphones, and pulled out her notes on Chelsie. Transported by the music, something suddenly clicked in her brain, and the words flowed freely:

Fifteen-year-old Chelsie Peterson, an exchange student from London, is many things, all of them surprising and wonderful. She's a poet, an animal lover, a songwriter, and an awesome guitarist. She also knows a lot about government because her father is a British diplomat. He works here in

New York and also travels a lot to other parts of the world.

"I'm proud of what my dad does," Chelsie says, "because he's working to end hunger and bring peace to the world. I'd like to do that, too, but in my own way, through writing and music."

She's already made an excellent start. A song of hers on homelessness was named "Best Student Song" in England last year. One of the amazing things about Chelsie, though, is her modesty. "Everybody at I. H. is good at something," she says. "I just happen to love writing and music."

Barbie was extremely proud of what she wrote. And she had done it in less than 150 words. When Chelsie called, they read their compositions to each other. Chelsie was really impressed, but she was embarrassed by the part about her award. She wanted Barbie to take it out. But Barbie persuaded her to let it stay in. Chelsie's composition was excellent, too, full of vivid, descriptive words. Barbie couldn't believe that an essay about herself could sound so good.

After they got off the phone, Barbie sat at her

desk and gazed out the window at New York's twinkling night-lights. Now she had two new friends, she thought — if only she could keep from losing Lara over the incident with the Australian girl.

Chapter 7

Process of Elimination

The next day, Thursday, was the first full day of school. Barbie left extra early to see if she could get a list of all the foreign students' names before classes started. Maybe she could find the Australian girl that way. There was only a handful of kids waiting by the glass front doors when she arrived. Barbie knocked on the door until a short, compact figure appeared inside. He was wearing charcoal-gray coveralls, a blue denim shirt, and hard-toed work boots the color of butterscotch. Sandy-brown hair poked out like straw from under his cap. His name, sewn in red script on his coveralls, was BORIS PUGACHEV. Below it, in even tinier red letters, was his title: CHIEF CUSTODIAN. Mr. Pugachev was the school janitor.

"What is it, please?" the man called through the door in a thick foreign accent that Barbie couldn't quite place. Was it Russian? German? Barbie wasn't sure. Whatever it was, it sure wasn't French.

"Hi! Can you please let me in?" Barbie asked.

Lifting his glasses off his nose like an old drawbridge, the janitor squinted nearsightedly at his watch. "It is too early, my little pachoochkie."

"Ple-ease," begged Barbie. "I need to go to the office. I'm trying to locate another student."

The janitor cracked open the door just wide enough to insert his boot against the jamb. "In America, everything is rush, rush, rush," he said, wrinkling his brow. "You cannot do this later?"

Barbie shook her head vehemently. "My schedule's sooo tight! I've got no free periods. If I can't do it now, I'll have to skip lunch or wait till after school."

"Skipping lunch is very bad idea," Mr. Pugachev said. "Is this emergency?"

"Not exactly," Barbie admitted. "It's just that I'm trying to help someone out."

"This is friend?"

"Yes."

Mr. Pugachev repositioned his glasses on his nose. He pursed his lips and thought for a moment. Barbie could sense he was wavering. "Ple-e-ease," she repeated.

"Okay," he said. "By me this is okey-dokey case." That said, he let Barbie in.

Once inside, Barbie scurried off to the office. Her luck couldn't have been better. Rubia Santana, Principal Simmons's secretary, happily informed her that a directory of all I. H. students had been mailed out yesterday to every student. But if Barbie absolutely needed to see one now, she added, she could check the copy posted outside the library.

The escalators were still on the fritz, and the elevators, at the far end of the building, were in dubious working order. So Barbie decided to hoof it up to the third-floor library. Again, she was in luck. The directory was in alphabetical order, but a separate column listed the nationality and faculty adviser of each foreign student. In a short time,

Barbie was able to identify three Australian students: Tori Burns, Glenda Eastwick, and Bradley Wilshire. The third name was easy to eliminate. That left just two choices — Tori and Glenda. Barbie smiled inwardly. The odds were looking good. She just might be able to find this girl.

BRRRINNG! The morning bells rang, and the school doors were flung open wide. Hastily, Barbie scribbled down the information on her two prime candidates. Then she slipped the notes in her backpack and headed for the stairwell. She thanked her stars that her first-period class was only one more floor up. Her legs were totally maxed out by that mad dash up three flights.

Outside her first-period classroom, she heard a voice calling out her name.

"Barbie! Barbie!"

Glancing in the direction of the sound, she saw Chelsie approaching.

"Hi, Chelsie," she said. "Coming in here, I hope?"

"Sorry, no. I've got French down the hall." She cocked her head toward the classroom. "What's in there?"

Barbie made a sour face. "History — ugh!"

"It can't be that bad," the English girl replied.

"Not for you, maybe. But it's definitely not my favorite subject. Somehow I can't seem to keep all those wars and peace treaties straight. I never could see why people couldn't get along in the first place."

"I'm with you on that," remarked Chelsie. "But my dad always says you can't help people stop arguing unless you know why they started. That's why I fancy history, anyway."

"I guess you're right."

"Hey, wait a minute, Ms. Roberts! I just wrote a composition about you, remember? Didn't you tell me it's a snap to learn a script?"

"That's different."

"I'll bet it's not so different," said Chelsie. "It's just about how much you want to."

"Maybe you're right," said Barbie, grinning.

Chelsie backed down the hall, clutching a loose-leaf notebook to her chest. "If you ever need help with history, we can always study together."

"Thanks, Chelsie," said Barbie. "I may take you up on that."

"By the way," Chelsie added, "I loved what you wrote about me for English. I only wish half of it were true."

"Vice versa."

Chelsie waved. "See you second period."

"See you."

The morning passed pretty smoothly for Barbie. First-period history went better than anticipated. Her teacher, Mr. Budge, seemed very knowledgeable but he did come across as, well, a little odd. He talked in a monotone and spent most of the class drawing sweeping arrows between names and dates on the blackboard. The problem was he never erased anything. So it wasn't long before everything he wrote disappeared under a thicket of chalk lines. When Barbie looked down at her own notes, she saw that they, too, resembled a heap of spaghetti. Even more bewildering, Mr. Budge spent the last minutes of the class lecturing about the importance of personal cleanliness. Nobody could figure out what any of this had to do with American history.

In second-period English, Mr. Toussaint collected all the compositions, mixed them up, then passed them out again. He had each student read an essay aloud, substituting the name "Fluffy" or "Sluggo" for the actual name of the girl or boy described. Then he asked the class to try to guess, just from the description, who "Fluffy" or "Sluggo" might really be. This was especially hard because nobody knew anyone else that well, and all anybody had to go on were the clues from the text. Like yesterday, there were tons of surprises and a lot of good-natured ribbing and laughter.

Barbie loved the way Mr. Toussaint taught English. She wished she could take every course he gave at I. H. When he reminded the class, at the bell, that the school newspaper would be staffing up next week, Barbie decided then and there that she was going to try out for it.

In the hallway, Barbie and Chelsie talked about their chances of getting on the newspaper staff. "You probably have a better chance of getting on, I'd say," the English girl replied with a smile.

"You mean you're going out for the paper, too? That's excellent!"

"Great minds think alike," she said, laughing.

Barbie's eyes danced with new possibilities. "Wouldn't it be great if we both made it? We could become a pair of crusading reporters!"

"That's right," said Chelsie, lofting a pen in the air. "Champions of free speech. You know, 'Writing equals honesty—' "

"—'equals truth,'" finished Barbie. "Yeah, I know. I've got that burned into my brain, too."

The two girls drifted down the hall together, laughing. Then they parted ways at the elevator.

As the day wore on, Barbie was disappointed that she hadn't managed to hook up with Lara yet. The European girl, who was taking a lot of advanced subjects, didn't seem to be in any of her classes. Luckily, she did have Chelsie in her English and math classes; Ana in her biology class; and Chelsie, Nichelle, and Ana shared a table with her during fourth-period lunch.

She liked all of these girls, especially because she couldn't imagine a more different set of personalities. Poetic Chelsie was sweet and shy (even though she did seem able to open up to Barbie). Ana was a no-nonsense, what-you-see-is-what-you-get type.

Barbie guessed that she pushed herself extremely hard when it came to athletics and didn't like settling for second best. Nichelle, on the other hand, was clever and funny and easy to be around. Not a hint of tension in her nature. But after just one lunch period, Barbie got the clear impression that Nichelle was also a person who thought and cared deeply about many different things. Barbie wasn't at all surprised to discover that, among her many hidden talents, Nichelle was quite a successful teenage model.

By the time seventh period, the last period of the day, rolled around, Barbie had given up hope of sharing any classes with Lara. Seventh period was phys ed, and Lara was not there. All the girls in the class were sitting on the high-gloss wooden floor waiting for Ms. Krieger, the teacher, to take attendance. She was a petite woman with button eyes and a cloud of frizzy black hair, and her voice was so tiny and squeaky that she had to use a megaphone to make herself heard above the general buzz in the room.

"Please raise your hand and respond to your name when I call you," the gym teacher instructed.

New York, Here We Come

As Ms. Krieger took roll, Barbie folded her legs underneath her and amused herself by counting the rows of bricks that lay between the bleachers and the ceiling.

Ms. Krieger droned on:

"Rosalia Diaz."

"Here!"

"Celeste Drury."

"Present!"

"Glenda Eastwick."

"G'day!"

Glenda Eastwick? That name! That accent! Was it the Aussie? Barbie swiveled around. A willowy redhead with a freckled face and a mouth full of braces had her hand in the air. *Drat!* thought Barbie in dismay. It wasn't her girl. But that meant her Aussie had to be Tori Burns, or it was no one else at I. H.!

Chapter 8

As the Cookie Crumbles

"**H**urry up, Barbie!" Terri said. "You'll be late for Selma."

Barbie whirled around her room like a blond tornado. She snatched a pair of black leather boots to go with her black slacks and light pink sweater. "There. I think I'm ready now."

Sam's had just opened for dinner when they arrived. There were already a few regulars at the bar and half a dozen couples in the main dining area, scanning menus. Harry, the head waiter, greeted Terri warmly, then turned to Barbie. "Good evening, Ms. Roberts," he said. "I believe your party has arrived. She's in the back dining area with Mr. Jenner."

Barbie followed Terri as she wound her way through the restaurant to a quiet corner in the rear. There, seated beside Sam in a plush velvet booth, was a plump woman with heavily lacquered copper-colored hair. She had piercing gray eyes and long, thickly mascaraed lashes. She was decked out like a jewelry showcase. Big, spangly earrings dangled from her ears. Silver bracelets jangled on her wrists. And a diamond-studded iguana brooch glittered on her blouse. Selma struck Barbie as a person who never came unprepared for anything. Her leather pocketbook, nestled at her feet, was as big as a mailbag and just as stuffed with papers. Three lime-green cell phones, two fountain pens, and a bulging leather date book lay within her easy reach on the table. As Terri and Barbie approached, she was going over the menu with Sam and sucking on a lollipop that was shaped like a whistle.

Sam rose and gave Terri a kiss hello. Then he kissed Barbie on the cheek and said, "Hi, sweetie. It's nice to have you here again. You look very pretty, by the way."

Selma yanked the lollipop out of her mouth with an audible pop. "Sam," she scolded in her scratchy voice. "You're such a liar. What do you know from pretty? She's not pretty. She's beautiful."

"Oops, I stand corrected," Sam said. "Selma, may I present the beautiful Barbie Roberts. And, Barbie, I'd like you to meet the one and only Selma Devine."

Barbie blushed and smiled politely. "Hi, Selma," she said, extending her hand. "I'm pleased to meet you in person."

"The feeling's mutual," said the agent. "Now, c'mon," she added. "Everybody sit down, quick. Just watching you is making my ankles swell."

Sam stayed just long enough to suggest a few specialties for dinner, then left to tend to other customers. Terri and Selma chatted for a while, catching up on old acquaintances. Terri explained to Barbie that, before becoming an agent, Selma had run a photographic service that sold news photographs to newspapers and magazines around the world. Selma had been the one who had given Terri her first job as a photojournalist. In fact, Terri had met Sam while covering a royal wedding in Europe for Selma. He was catering a banquet, and she was snapping pictures. Even after Selma had switched over to representing actors, they'd all stayed close friends.

Barbie was fascinated by the story. She also knew that Terri had another reason for telling the tale. By slowly introducing her into the conversation with Selma, Terri was helping her feel more comfortable. Barbie loved her for doing that. Terri was always so considerate and thoughtful.

When the appetizers arrived, Terri said, "I guess I'll leave you two alone to eat and talk business. I'm going to go and pester the owner of this joint, but I'll be back before dessert. By the way, I hear the banana cream pie is absolutely fabulous tonight."

After Terri left, Selma deposited her lollipop stick in an ashtray. Then she searched through her oversized pocketbook and took out a fresh whistle lollipop. "Here, take it. It's my one vice. This one's watermelon. I have them flown in from Switzerland." She chuckled. "They're called Swisstle Pops. They actually whistle."

Barbie laughed and took the pop. "I'll save it for later," she said.

"Good idea. They helped me stop smoking. Now I don't go anywhere without them."

"It's terrific you stopped smoking," Barbie said. "It's a horrible habit. I know I'm never going to start."

"Smart kid."

Barbie and Selma polished off their appetizers, two heavenly tasting bowls of mint-'n'-melon soup. As the waiter placed the main course — duckling in orange sauce — before them, Selma leaned over and pulled a thick folder out of her bag. "So here's the deal, Barbie," she said. "You tell me if you're interested, okay?"

Barbie's heart was in her mouth. "Okay."

"Most of my clients are veteran actors — people who've worked a long time in film and TV. But these days directors are looking for new and younger faces. So if I'm going to stay competitive, I've got to find those faces. You follow?"

"Absolutely."

"Now I have a hunch — and it's only a hunch, mind you — that with a little training and experience, you might be one of those new faces."

Barbie felt faint. "You're saying this for real? Do you really think I have a chance?"

"I do," replied Selma. "But chances are only as good as what you make of them. You can't expect to start at the top. The bottom line is: If you'll work with me, I'll work with you."

"Yes!" said Barbie, nearly knocking over her water glass. "I'd love you as my agent."

"Good, that's settled, then." She handed Barbie the folder. "If you look in there, you'll find a script. It's for a commercial. You've heard of Crumbly Cookies?"

"They're chocolate chiperrific!" said Barbie, reciting the slogan from the television ads.

"You got it. Well, the director of those — and other — commercials is Lee Quigley. He also does a lot of TV series and feature films. Did you happen to see *Dance Till Tomorrow* or *Screaming in the Rain* or *Alien Love Boat*? Big movies. That was Quigley. So even getting into a commercial by him could lead to a bigger break. That's why I want you to take this script home and study it as if it were Shakespeare."

"You're talking about a speaking part?"

"You bet — the part of Chipper Girl. Quigley told me he wants a sweet, wholesome, blond type. And that's you. The audition is a week from Saturday. Can you do it?"

"Yikes! That's only eight days."

"I know. It's short notice. And you'll have to fit this in on top of your regular schoolwork. But you'll never be an actor if you can't deal with pressure."

Barbie looked Selma squarely in the eyes. "I can do this. I know I can do this."

"That's what I wanted to hear," Selma said, beaming. "There's also some decent money in it for you if this works out, money you can put aside for college. And, of course, a little money for me." Selma took a bite of her duck. "Mmm! This is scrumptious." She motioned to Barbie to start eating. "Letting an incredible meal go cold is definitely not part of this deal."

"I never imagined I'd get an audition so soon," Barbie confessed.

"Look, I'm gonna help you as best as I can. And, remember, whether you get the part or not, the experience will be invaluable. Even a defeat can sometimes be a disguised victory." She gave Barbie a wink. "Now, eat up! Sam will throw me out on my rear if I keep you from tasting his food."

Barbie grinned and returned to her meal. Selma was a real character, just like Sam had said. But Barbie liked her style. And despite her rough edges, she clearly had a good heart. She was like a fairy godmother who had popped into Barbie's life out of thin air. Now she was waving a magic wand over her head and asking her to make a wish. It seemed almost too good to be true.

When Terri returned for dessert, Sam joined them again. Then Selma reached into her magic bag of tricks and pulled out a photo album. And they all had fun looking at pictures of Terri and Sam and Selma when they were younger.

Chapter 9

Tori's Story

Mr. Toussaint was passing back the English compositions when Chelsie leaned across the aisle and quietly dropped a note onto Barbie's desk. It said:

Congratulations on your audition! I know you'll be excellent. I'm so excited for you! I just can't believe one of my friends is going to be on the telly. (Oops, I'm forgetting! In case you don't know, "telly" is Britspeak for TV.)

Barbie blushed a little. The minute she'd gotten home last night, she'd called everyone she knew to tell them the wonderful news. Her sisters. Her friends back in California. Then her new friends in New York. She'd even stayed up way past midnight writing a long e-mail to her parents in China. Now she was feeling a little embarrassed about last night's giddy gushiness. After all, it was only an audition. She hadn't won the part yet.

Of all her I. H. friends, she'd talked to Chelsie the longest — for more than an hour. She'd also chatted briefly with Ana and Nichelle. All of them had been thrilled at her good fortune. The only school-mate she hadn't managed to reach was Lara. Barbie gave a wistful sigh.

Suddenly a thought occurred to her. "Say, Chelsie, do you happen to know a girl named Tori Burns?"

"I hear someone talking in this class!" grumbled Mr. Toussaint. "If you can't share it with everyone, please don't say it to anyone."

Chelsie looked at Barbie and nodded silently. Then she mouthed the words, "Talk to me later."

The period went swiftly. After returning the compositions (Chelsie got an A, Barbie an A -), Mr. Toussaint handed out photocopies of a short mystery story. "Read it," he said. "You'll notice that I've left out the last page. That's so you can write your own ending. On Monday, I'll let you see what the author actually wrote." He paused. "Oh, and while I'm thinking of it, I'd like to put in another plug for the newspaper. The first meeting of the staff will be on Monday in Room 712. I'm also happy to announce that Principal Simmons has given me the go-ahead to create an I. H. internet website that will be linked to the newspaper. Anyone interested in these activities should attend the meeting."

In between periods, Barbie escorted Chelsie to her history class. "So, you know Tori Burns?"

"Australian? Blond, wears her hair in ponytails? Carries skates around with her everywhere?"

"That's her."

"She's in my last-period biology class."

"Great! Where's that?"

"Third floor — Room 329."

Barbie made a mental note of the room number. "Chelsie, could you do me a favor?" she asked.

"Sure."

"Could you tell her that the girl she met on the

subway — the one who was trying to get the old guy a seat — wants to see her?"

Chelsie stared at her quizzically. "That's the message?"

"No, there's more. Tell her to wait for me outside biology. I need to talk to her. It's kinda important."

"Okay," said Chelsie, looking slightly mystified.

After seventh-period gym, Barbie scooted up to the third floor, where she found Chelsie leaning against the lockers outside Room 329.

"Hi, Chelsie," she said, panting heavily. "Tori here?" She gazed up and down the hallway, then into the empty biology lab.

Chelsie shook her head. "She left two minutes ago. She said she had to make a three-thirty rock-climbing class."

"Oh, no! Did she say anything else?"

"She said she remembered you and told me to tell you hi. And she said if you really needed to talk to her, you could meet her at her class."

"Did she say where it was?"

"That's easy. The Chelsea Piers — just like my name, only spelled differently."

"Perfect. You're the best, Chelsie!" Barbie cried.

She wheeled and headed down the hall. "Got to run now. I'll call you tonight."

"See you," said Chelsie, waving good-bye in bewilderment.

Barbie hopped a cab uptown to the huge sports complex known as the Chelsea Piers. The facility was like an all-weather playland overlooking the Hudson River. It had an indoor swimming pool, a health club, tennis courts, an ice-skating rink, a golf-driving range, an obstacle course for skateboarding and in-line skating, and an amazing rock-climbing wall. If you were into any kind of sports — from regular to extreme — the Chelsea Piers had something for you.

Checking the directory of activities, Barbie located Tori's rock-climbing class. As she entered the big room, the Australian girl was in a safety harness and methodically scaling a dizzying rock wall that was over twenty feet tall. Tori was amazingly strong and surefooted. She never hesitated, never looked down, and never looked the least bit scared. Even more remarkable, she appeared to be making this demanding ascent despite a large and painful-looking bruise below her left knee. When she reached the top, she held on with one hand, thrust the other ecstatically into the air, and shouted, "Yes!"

Suddenly she caught sight of Barbie. "Crikey! You did come by, mate!" she called down. "Good seeing you. Be off here in a sec." Tori made her way down the wall. Then she detached her safety harness, thanked the instructor, and walked over toward Barbie, limping slightly.

"Wow! You're a serious climber," Barbie said. "Do you do this often?"

"Every chance I get," Tori replied, mopping her forehead with a towel. "Next to in-line skating and skateboarding, it's about my absolute favorite thing." She draped the towel around her neck and tugged it taut with her hands. "Chelsie said your name's Barbie, right?"

"Right. And you're Tori?"

"That's me."

Barbie smiled awkwardly. "Guess it's kinda weird that here we are introducing ourselves days after we actually met."

"Yeah, names are stupid, anyway," Tori said. "You don't really need 'em to know who a person is."

"That's what I think, too."

"For instance," Tori went on. "I knew you were fair-dinkum the second you stood up for that old guy."

"Fair *whatsit*?" Barbie said, grinning. "Is that good or bad?"

"Crikey! It's, like, one of the best compliments you can get from an Aussie."

"Gee, thanks, then. But, you know, I wouldn't have gotten anywhere if you hadn't come along."

"Nah, I just hate to see a boofhead taking advantage of someone else." Tori winced. "Walk with me. I need to sit down somewhere."

Tori and Barbie found a bench by the locker room. Tori stretched her injured leg out and sighed. "Now, what's up?" she said to Barbie. "Chelsie said you wanted to see me, but she didn't know why."

Barbie took a deep breath and started to tell Tori about the loss of Lara's paint box. When she got to the part about Lara's suspicion that Tori took it, Tori's face reddened.

"Wait a minute!" Tori said angrily. "That's totally

wacko. I didn't steal her paint box. I was the one who got it back!"

"You what?"

"You heard. I rescued it — and nearly broke my leg doing it." She rubbed the tender spot below her knee.

Barbie's eyes widened. "What happened?"

"Well, I was skating in front of school and I saw your friend leave her box by the sculpture and go inside. That was a pretty dumb thing to do. So I sort of watched out from a distance. Sure enough, this guy — he must've been about twenty — skated by, stopped, and grabbed the box. There was nobody around but him and me. So when he took off, I took off after him. When he saw I was on his tail, he dropped the box like a hot coal. Then I scooped it up and kept on chasing him, hoping to find a cop."

"And that's when Lara saw you, right?"

"I guess. But she only saw half the picture."

"I knew there was a good explanation," Barbie said. "Did you catch the guy?"

"No, he got away. I hit a bump and went head

over heels. I was so mad. I was almost at Fourteenth Street by then. It took me another hour to limp back to school."

"And the box?"

"You mean she hasn't got it yet?"

"I dunno. Maybe. I haven't talked with her."

"I gave it to Poogy."

"Poogy?"

"You know, Mr. Pugachev, the janitor. When I got back to I. H., I gave it to him to put in the lost and found. I'm sure she's got it by now."

Barbie grinned from ear to ear. "Tori, you don't know how happy this makes me."

"Me, too," Tori replied. "I didn't realize how close I'd come to getting turned in to the cops. Thanks for believing in me."

Barbie laughed. "I knew immediately that you were fair-dinkum, too."

Chapter 10

Murder (Almost) in Room 712!

A ll weekend long Barbie studied the script for the Crumbly Cookies commercial. She had Terri ask her lines. She had Sam test her. She called up Selma and practiced her part over the telephone. She videotaped six hours of children's TV programs so that she could view every cookie commercial on the air.

On Sunday, she went out and bought a shopping bag full of different brands of chocolate chip cookies. Then she blindfolded herself and had Terri serve her random pieces until that she could detect which ones were Crumbly's simply by taste or smell.

"You can't act if you can't relate," she explained to Terri. "And I've got to be able to relate to these cookies by next Saturday."

"Don't you, um, think you're going just a little overboard?" Sam finally asked late Sunday night when he noticed that Barbie was sitting in the kitchen snapping cookies in half just to hear the sound they made.

"Uh-uh," she said. "This is crucial. See, in the script, Chipper Girl has to make the 'extra crunchability' sound. She's a superhero who flies around making sure kids are happy with their cookies."

"Right," said Sam. "You've read me the script, remember?"

"So, anyway, when she learns that Brand X Boy has been trying to pass off his cookies as better, she challenges him to a 'crunchability' duel."

"Right. I remember that, too."

"Then she takes a bite of a Crumbly Cookie, and its 'extra crunchability' wins hands down."

"So?"

"So I need to be able to make that sound. I need to understand the essence of 'crunchability.'"

"Okay," said Sam, chuckling. "You do whatever you have to do. Only don't neglect your homework."

Before going to sleep, Barbie dialed Lara, but nobody was home yet. So she resigned herself to waiting until tomorrow to tell Lara the good news about her paint box.

All in all, it had been a magical week, she thought as she turned out the lights. Could it possibly get any better? She sighed. Only if her audition went well.

On Monday, Barbie and Ana were sitting in third-period biology lab with a cow's eyeball staring up at them from a tray when the public-address system crackled. "Attention! Attention, students!" a voice barked. "This is Assistant Principal Merlin speaking with the morning announcements." He paused. Everyone heard a big sneeze building up in the background.

"*Ah . . . ah . . . ah . . . CHOOO!*" it thundered. Mr. Merlin blew his nose, then cleared his throat. "Pardon me," he said. "That was not one of the morning announcements." He blew his nose again and started all over: "Attention, students. For anyone interested in singing, there will be a meeting of the mixed chorus after school in Room 111. The boys' soccer team will hold their first meeting on the field at three-thirty. Lastly, any students interested in joining the school newspaper or website should go to Room 712 after seventh period. In conclusion, I'd like to leave you with this thought: Every day is a blank page in the notebook of life. What will you write upon yours today? This is Assistant Principal Merlin. Over and out."

The P.A. system sputtered some more, then was silent. Ana glanced down at the cow's eyeball and shuddered. "Yuck, Barbie! I can't stand to look at this." As Ms. Clayton drew a diagram of the eyeball on the board, Ana covered the specimen in front of her with a paper towel. "There, that's better!"

Barbie poked her friend in the ribs. "C'mon, Ana. Where's your scientific spirit? Biology is amazing. Don't you want to know how an eye really works?"

"I can learn everything I need from a textbook, thank you," replied Ana. "At least a book doesn't creep you out by watching back."

Barbie giggled. "Hey, Ana?" she said, changing the subject. "You've got Mr. Toussaint, too, right?"

"First period."

"Anybody in your class going out for the paper?"

Ana scratched her head. "I dunno. Did he do those interview compositions in your class?"

"Uh-huh."

"Well, after we got ours back, he stopped me after class and asked me if I'd like to write about sports."

"He did? I'm jealous. He must really like your writing."

"Nah," Ana said. "He only gave me a B minus. I'm sure he did it because he thinks it'll make me write better. And he knows how I feel about sports, because of the composition that was written on me. He told me it's always better to have a reporter who's an expert on what she's writing."

"Makes sense." Barbie tapped her pencil on the surface of the table that she and Ana shared. "You gonna join? Chelsie's interested and so am I."

"Maybe," Ana said.

"C'mon," cajoled Barbie. "It'll be fun, you'll see. You and me and Chelsie."

"And Nichelle," added Ana.

"Nichelle? I didn't know she was interested!"

"Big-time. She wants to write a column on style and fashion."

"Wow! That's perfect for her." A mischievous grin spread across Barbie's face. She whipped off the paper towel from the cow's eye.

"Ugh! What are you doing, girl?" Ana asked. "Put that back."

"Please go with us after school, Ana — ple-e-ease! It'll be so much fun."

"Will you cover the dish again?"

"Promise."

"Okay," relented Ana. "I'll stop by."

By three-thirty about fifteen kids had packed into Room 712. It had a small blackboard, no windows, and a bunch of computers and printers still in their boxes. Some kids had found chairs; others were sitting on the radiator along a cinder-block wall. Still others, including Barbie, Chelsie, Nichelle, and Ana, sat on the floor. So did Fletcher from English class, and Randall, the talented and cute cartoonist.

A few minutes later Mr. Toussaint walked in the

room. He immediately took off his suit jacket and rolled up his shirtsleeves. Then he asked Fletcher to fetch a fan so that no one would suffocate.

"Sorry about the space," he said. "It's the largest I could get. But you'll get used to it. In fact, you'll probably come to call it your second home."

Mr. Toussaint spent a few minutes outlining the goals of the newspaper and website. He said that its purpose was to communicate not only to the I. H. student body, but, through the website, to the whole world. He spoke, as he did in class, about the honesty that writing required, and of the special responsibility journalists had to respect the truth. Then he passed out a sheet that listed the different jobs that needed to be done, and asked everyone to indicate which ones they might like to do.

As the sheet was going around, there was a knock on the door.

"Enter!" boomed Mr. Toussaint. "The more the merrier."

In walked a tall and beautiful girl with a thick, dark brown braid running down the length of her back. She was carrying a book bag and a large sketch pad.

"Lara!" shouted Barbie, Chelsie, and Nichelle in unison. They waved their hands. "Over here!" The girls all looked at each other with a mixture of delight and astonishment. Nobody had any idea that Lara was interested in journalism.

"Thank you for coming, Ms. Morelli-Strauss," Mr. Toussaint said to Lara. "I'm glad Mr. Harris convinced you to come. He told me about your considerable artistic talents. We can really use a good illustrator and designer."

Lara smiled and made her way haltingly over to her friends. Barbie was so excited to see her again. After she'd sat down, Lara hurriedly apologized to Barbie for not getting in touch with her sooner. Her parents had unexpectedly decided to take her to Boston to meet an old friend of theirs who taught fine arts at Harvard University. The friend, who was the head of the university's admissions committee, had been deeply interested in seeing some of Lara's artwork. It had been an opportunity Lara simply couldn't pass up.

For the rest of the meeting, Mr. Toussaint talked about possible story ideas and deadlines for the first issue. He also proposed that the group come up with a name for the newspaper and website. After a lengthy discussion, everyone agreed that the names proposed by Nichelle — *Generation Beat* and *Generation Beat Web* — were the best.

"I think they really capture what we're trying to do here," Mr. Toussaint said. "They identify our school. They say we're hip — like world beat music. And they also say that our 'beat' as journalists is the world. Very clever, Nichelle."

"Excellent!" Barbie said.

"I love it!" cried Chelsie.

"Good, then it's settled. That's what we'll call our publications."

Mr. Toussaint was starting to wind things down when there was a loud *click-clack, click-clack, click-clack* in the hall. It got louder and louder. The room got quieter and quieter as everyone tried to figure out what the noise was.

Suddenly, the noise stopped. The door burst open, and there stood Tori on skates. "Sorry I'm late, Mr. Toussaint! My French teacher wanted to see me—"

Tori didn't get a chance to finish her sentence, because Lara stood up and pointed an accusatory finger at her. "That's the girl! She's the one who stole my paint box!"

Mr. Toussaint looked befuddled. Everyone in the room looked puzzled, including Tori. Barbie sensed that something had gone horribly wrong.

"I think you'd better check your facts before you speak, mate," said Tori angrily.

"Just hold it, girls!" Mr. Toussaint said. "This sounds like a private matter. Can't it wait until after our meeting?"

Lara and Tori nodded, eyeing each other suspiciously. Tori took a seat at the far side of the room.

The meeting went on for another twenty minutes. Then, when it was almost ready to break up, there was a hesitant knock on the door.

"Come in," said Mr. Toussaint, looking a bit irritated at yet another disruption.

It was Poogy. Under his arm was Lara's paint box.

"Please excuse for this interrupting," he apologized to Mr. Toussaint. "But Mr. Harris thought I might find Lara Morelli-Strauss here. Is she at this meeting?"

Lara stood up, looking bewildered.

"Tori gave this box to me a few days ago," Poogy

said to Lara. "I am having it in lost and found since before the weekend. See, it has your name right in corner. I thought you would be missing it and pick it up right away. It is very beautiful box. But you did not stop by. So I told Principal Simmons, and she asked me to see Mr. Harris. Here," he said, handing Lara the box. "Now it is safely returned."

Lara gazed back and forth from the box to Tori. "You mean, you turned it in? You didn't steal it? But — I saw you skating away with it!"

By this point, Mr. Toussaint had abandoned hope of continuing with the meeting. Everyone's attention, including Poogy's, was riveted on the two girls as Tori angrily explained to Lara what had happened.

"Maybe it wasn't worth getting this after all," she said, rolling up her baggy jeans to display the bruise. "I should've let that bloke make off with your box!"

The normally cool Lara looked flustered and up-set. "I am so sorry," she said. "I thought the wrong thing about you. But — perhaps you can under-stand what it looked like to me. After all, I did not know you. I just saw you skating away."

Tori thought about this. "Fair enough," she said at last. "I guess I can see that. I s'pose I did look like I was nicking it, eh? It's a good thing someone had faith in me." She looked at Barbie.

Barbie was limp with relief, grinning from ear to ear. Everything was going to be okay.

Tori stuck out a hand. "No hard feelings, then, Lara?" she said. "It's all in the past now."

Lara smiled warmly as she shook Tori's hand. "No hard feelings. And I thank you so much for saving my beloved paint box. I never should have left it sitting there by itself." She pulled one of her hand-painted postcards out of the box and handed it to Tori.

Tori looked at it. "This is bonzer!" she said. "D'you make it?"

"Bonzer?" Lara echoed in confusion.

"Sorry. Australian. It's great."

"Ah," said Lara. "Thank you."

Poogy cleared his throat and began backing out of the room.

"Oh! I am sorry," said Lara. "I forgot to thank you, too! You came all the way up here to find me. That was very nice."

"Is no trouble," said Poogy, looking a little embarrassed by the uproar he'd caused. "Back to my boiler," he said, exiting quickly out the door.

"Well," said Mr. Toussaint, "this just shows that we don't have to go to Broadway to see good theater. Is everyone okay now?"

Everyone nodded happily.

"Good," Mr. Toussaint said. "Because I was going to suggest that we all have a small celebration for the birth of *Generation Beat*."

"And the return of Lara's box," added Nichelle.

"Sure — that, too," said Mr. Toussaint. "Is Eatz okay with everyone? The sodas and pizzas are on me."

A shout of joy rocked the room. And Mr. Toussaint's rookie staff members headed out for a feast of music and munchies.

Chapter 11

Chipper Girl Versus Brand X Boy

As the week wore on, Barbie grew more and more nervous about her audition. What made things more bearable than they might otherwise have been was the fact that all her new friends were pitching in to help. Even Lara and Tori, once they got to know each other, were able to put their awkward misunderstanding behind them and work together.

On Wednesday night, Selma arranged for a full rehearsal at Terri and Sam's apartment. Tori and Ana cleared a large open area in the living room, while Nichelle and Selma made Barbie up to fit Chipper Girl's description. Then, while Terri and Sam adjusted the lamps for effective lighting, Selma directed a run-through of the script with Barbie playing Chipper Girl and Nichelle in the role of Brand X Boy. Lara videotaped the short playlet using Barbie's video camera. Then everybody gathered round as Selma replayed the tape on the VCR and critiqued Barbie's performance.

"You're great in the close-ups, honey," she told Barbie. "You really know how to play to the camera with your facial expressions. Believe me, that's the name of the game in TV."

Barbie sensed Selma was holding something back. "But?" she said.

"But even though you're playing a superhero here, the real hero of this whole shebang is the cookie. So when you get into the whole 'crunchability' thing, you gotta act like the cookie is the star, and you're just sort of playing a supporting role. Do you get me?"

"I think so," Barbie said.

"Good." Selma waved her hand above her head

in a small circle. "Okay, everyone. Let's take it from the top again. Places!" she called. "Ready? Action!"

By Saturday morning, Barbie was ready for her Crumbly Cookies audition to be over and done with. She'd dreamed the night before that she was in biology class with Ana, and Ms. Clayton was drawing a diagram of a chocolate chip cookie on the board. When Barbie looked down at her tray, there was a sinister-looking chocolate chip glaring up at her.

"You'll never catch me alive, Chipper Girl!" he yelled, and jumped out the window. Then Barbie had awakened.

The audition was at 10 A.M. on Madison Avenue and Forty-sixth Street.

Selma met her at the studio and escorted her onto the set, where she introduced her to the director. Lee Quigley was a round-faced man in his fifties with extremely hairy arms and a potbelly. He was the kind of man who laughed at everything vaguely humorous, whether it was really funny or not. But he was also the kind of person who made you feel as if you were the only person in the room and he was just thrilled to be in your company.

"Selma, you never looked lovelier," he said, chucking her under the chin. "So, you've brought me your newest starlet, huh?"

"Lee, this is Barbie Roberts — the girl I was talking to you about."

"Ah, yes. Pleased to meet you, Barbie," the director said, shaking her hand. "You've read the script, I hope?"

"Yes, sir."

"Excellent! Now, if you don't mind, I'd like you to wait in the green room over there with the other candidates. Our lighting and makeup people will meet you there to take care of you."

"Great!" said Barbie, and she headed off to the room the director had indicated.

In the green room were five other girls — all taller than Barbie, all blond, and all beautiful. One of them sat coolly in a chair, blowing on her nails. She didn't seem in the least bit anxious. Another was not making eye contact with anyone. She had her face buried in the script. Two others were making strenuous efforts at conversation, discussing something neutral like where to go to buy the best secondhand clothes. The fifth girl seemed almost too twitchy for words. Barbie certainly hoped she would calm down a little, if only for her own health.

After the lighting, makeup, and costume people came in to check the girls out, the director's assistant called them to audition one by one. Barbie was the last to perform, after the twitchy blond. As she left the green room, Selma called out to her, "Break a leg, kid," the traditional way of wishing someone good luck in the theater.

Barbie smiled and waved to Selma.

Lee Quigley had Barbie run through the script twice. He stopped her once, during the "crunchability" scene, and had her make a half dozen different "crunchability" sounds. Barbie was really glad she'd practiced that a lot.

Afterward, the director asked Barbie to stand different ways, and asked the film crew to take a couple of close-ups with Barbie holding up a big package of Crumbly Cookies.

"Marvelous!" he said after the test was over. "You're a real natural."

Barbie beamed. She wondered how the other five girls had done.

"Would you mind going back into the green room for a minute, my dear?" the director said. "I'd like to consult with my colleagues."

Selma was standing back by the door to the green room. She gave Barbie a thumbs-up sign as she approached. "You were fabulous, honey!" she said. "He spent more time with you than he did with any of the others."

"He did?"

"Would I kid you?"

"Do you think I might get it?"

"You've got a fifty-fifty chance."

"You mean, there's another finalist?"

"Yeah, he liked this other girl, too. She seemed nervous at first. But when the lights went on she turned into a totally different person."

"Gee," said Barbie.

Selma opened the door to the green room. "Better get in there so these people can decide."

Inside the green room sat the twitchy girl. Barbie

had new respect for her. "I heard you did great," Barbie said.

"Thanks. I guess you did great, too, 'cause here you are, too."

"Yeah."

"This your first time auditioning?" the other girl asked.

Barbie nodded, then added, "In New York, at least."

"I've done this a lot," the other girl said. "I always get nervous beforehand, and it always, like, goes away when I'm actually acting. Funny, isn't it?"

"Yeah. It's amazing how a person can do stuff they never thought they could do when they have to."

"Yeah. I agree." The girl then picked up a fashion magazine and leafed through it slowly.

Barbie did the same. There wasn't much else to do.

Minutes later, the door opened. Lee Quigley poked his head in. "Barbie, may I speak with you, please?"

Barbie followed him back to the set. "I want to congratulate you on your work," he said. "It's rare that an actor — especially in something as abstract as a commercial — hits the nail on the head so well with so little direction."

Barbie glowed.

"Unfortunately, we've decided to go with Rachel, the other girl. It wasn't that she did that much better than you — she didn't — it was just that her 'crunchability' was really outstanding."

Barbie thought maybe she'd misheard. Maybe he hadn't said that he was hiring the other girl. Maybe it was Barbie's "crunchability" that was outstanding. Maybe . . . But she knew in her heart what she'd heard. She hadn't won the part. She knew that he was saying wonderful things about her and that she ought to listen, but she just couldn't. It hurt too much to think that she hadn't succeeded — particularly after Selma and Terri and Sam and all her friends had put in so much effort to help her. What would they think? What would they say when she told them that another girl would be playing Chipper Girl on TV?

Dimly she saw Selma standing in the shadows behind Lee Quigley. She seemed to be smiling.

Why is she smiling? Barbie wondered. *Her newest client — Barbie Roberts — has just bombed. How can she possibly be happy?*

Lee Quigley was saying something to her. What was it? Why was he smiling, too? What was he saying?

"... and I think you'd be just perfect for the Dominique Jeans commercials I'm shooting in a month. They're much more high profile. Far better exposure for you than a cookie spot." He paused. "I've talked it over with Selma, and we're going to offer you a contract. I'll messenger it up to you next week, along with the scripts. Okay?"

"You mean, you're offering me a part?"

"A better part, you dingbat!" Selma said, grinning. "See, I told you sometimes things work out okay even if they don't work out okay."

"Oh-my-gosh! Oh-my-gosh! I've got a part! I've got a part!"

"Then you accept?" Lee Quigley asked.

"Yes! I accept! I accept!"

Selma put her arm around Barbie's shoulders and gave her a hug. "Well, kiddo. What do you say we go home and tell everybody the fabulous news?"

Epilogue

Dear Skipper,

You guys would not believe what has happened in my life since I wrote you last! Everything is going at a New York pace — a mile a minute. Sam and Terri are the best substitute parents a girl could have. School is amazing. I've never met so many different kinds of kids in my whole life. And, guess what? I have friends already! Not just one or two, but FIVE friends. Their names are Lara, Tori, Nichelle, Ana, and Chelsie. I can already tell we're going to have fun all year. And guess what else? I'm going to be in a commercial! For Dominique Jeans. I wonder if they'll let me keep the jeans afterward?

Tell Stacie to stop reading those scary books at bedtime. And tell Kelly I sent her a little present yesterday. I miss you guys sooo much. But now I know that I'm going to be just fine here.

Love and hugs,
Barbie

TURN THE PAGE TO CATCH
THE LATEST BUZZ FROM
THE *GENERATION BEAT* NEWSPAPER.

GENERATI*N BEAT

NEW SCHOOL BUILDING OPENS

The school that has the whole world talking—the amazing International High School—is open for business!

Thousands of students from around the world streamed through its doors for the start of a new school year.

I.H.'s Principal Simmons worked hard to get the new building built, after watching students and teachers being crammed together for years. "It won't be long before the kinks in the building will be fixed," says the principal. "Meanwhile, just relax, use this time to make new friends, and take advantage of the school's awesome, exciting, city neighborhood."

A student body survey confirms that the school's location, set between Soho and Tribeca, are two of the coolest neighborhoods in the Big Apple.

Watch out! It's going to be an incredible year so — Enjoy!

CREATE YOUR OWN NEWSPAPER!

Working on a newspaper can be very exciting. If your school doesn't have one already, try starting your own. You can write about things that happen in your classroom, like field trips, tests, performances, and parties.

If you think writing for a newspaper sounds difficult, remember that you spend a large part of your school day writing. Once you learn how articles are written, you will see it's not that hard. Barbie and her friends met the challenge, and so can you!

A newspaper article should give the reader a lot of information in a simple and easy-to-read way. The following questions should be answered first:

1. Who is this article about?

2. What is this article about?

3. When did this event happen?

4. Where did this event happen?

5. Why did this event happen?

6. How did this event take place?

The *Generation Beat* writer answered the questions in the first few sentences.

1. Who: The people who will benefit from the new building are the students of International High School.

2. What: The article is about the new International High School building.

3. When: The new building opened at the start of a new school year.

4. Where: The new building is located on West Street, between the areas of Soho and Tribeca, in New York City.

5. Why: The new building was necessary because many new students have enrolled in International High School.

6. How: Principal Simmons raised money to build the new school.

When you are writing a news article, remember that your goal is to inform your readers.

- Provide as much important information as possible.

- Leave out any details that might be confusing.

- Write short, simple sentences.

- Try to summarize your article in the headline.

Try some of the following ideas to help you get started:

- Think of a title for your newspaper.

(Barbie's newspaper is called *Generation Beat*.)

- Brainstorm an idea to write about. (Choose something that is interesting to you.)

- Write a short article. Remember to write simple sentences and include only important details.

• Reread your article to see if you answered the "who, what, when, where, why, and how" questions.

• Also ask a friend to read what you've written. Don't be afraid to ask for criticism. Did they understand the point of your article? (Remember, your goal is to inform other people.)

Have fun! And always remember what Mr. Toussaint says:

WRITING=HONESTY=TRUTH!

DON'T MISS **GENERATI*N GIRL** #2:
BENDING THE RULES

When Tori's parents send her to high school in America, Tori wonders how she's ever going to get along with her crabby Aunt Tessa. But the discovery of a mysterious but talented artist, forbidden rooms, and strange comments from Tessa's parrot all lead to a big surprise.

CHECK OUT **generationgirl.com**
FOR MORE INFORMATION ON THE
GENERATION GIRLS!